THE BOSTON
BOMBERS

THE BOSTON
BOMBERS

William F. Russell

iUniverse LLC
Bloomington

THE BOSTON BOMBERS

iUniverse books may be ordered through booksellers or by contacting:

iUniverse LLC
1663 Liberty Drive
Bloomington, IN 47403
www.iuniverse.com
1-800-Authors (1-800-288-4677)

ISBN: 978-1-4917-1793-6 (sc)
ISBN: 978-1-4917-1794-3 (e)

Printed in the United States of America.

iUniverse rev. date: 12/11/2013

CONTENTS

Introduction...vii
Preface ix
Preamble xi

Chapter 1.   The New World 1
Chapter 2.   Parents Return to Chechnya............................... 9
Chapter 3.   Growing up in Boston 13
Chapter 4.   Watching the World Scene 20
Chapter 5.   Travel to Russia 23
Chapter 6.   Developing a Plan... 27
Chapter 7.   Making the Bomb.. 29
Chapter 8.   Let the Computer Help.. 30
Chapter 9.   Consolidation 31
Chapter 10.   Girls Girls Girls 33
Chapter 11.   News from Home 35
Chapter 12.   The Day Arrives.. 37
Chapter 13.   We Did It 42
Chapter 14.   Act Natural 43
Chapter 15.   The Aftermath 47
Chapter 16.   The Trial 49
Chapter 17.   Did We Learn Something? 57

About The Author 61
Addendum 63

INTRODUCTION

The country was stunned when on April 15, 2013 the Boston Marathon suffered a terrible bombing when innocent civilians' lives were lost forever and many lives were damaged. Two young homegrown Islamic terrorists bombed spectators and runners of the beloved marathon that has been a joyous rite of spring in Boston for many years. This blackest of days will surely go down in marathon history and we will forever pay tribute to the memories of lives lost or maimed there.

The shocking news immediately flashed around the world with condolences being received from many countries as the participants in this popular event, in the thousands with many seriously injured by the bombing, came from countries throughout the world.

This is a story about that event told in fictional form but including many of the actual incidences associated with the bombing.

There's much to be learned about these two young men who perpetrated this evil act. Why did they do it? Was it religious fervor alone or some other additional motivation? Will this terrible event answer questions that all are asking about a possible international conspiracy of Islam to take over America and the world?

There is currently much discussion about the motives of Islam. Many, including Pres. Obama, have said that Islam is a religion of peace. Cursory examination of the readily available and copious documentation, should easily lead to the conclusion that Islam is and has been for 1400 years a very important factor in fomenting international violence in the name of Islam.

In fact, is Islam truly a religion? Where it is empowered, it controls every element of the citizen's lives. What are the laws of the land? What are the standards of morality? These are controlled by the laws of Islam. Essentially all the laws of the land are controlled by Islam. Can this be only a religion?

No, it really is a theocracy in every sense of the word and should be recognized as such. It should not be granted the privileges of a religion including tax status relief.

Continuing investigations proceed by the FBI and the CIA to uncover what, if any, connections can be found with the Boston bombing as part of an international Islamic conspiracy.

PREFACE

This is a tragic story.

Tragic, because it tells the tale of the loss of life and limb, of hundreds of innocent women and children, out to enjoy the beloved Boston Marathon, on a sunny day in the beautiful city of Boston, Massachusetts. It is a tale of two Islamic zealots who perpetrated this horrible disaster. These were two boys growing up in America who were radicalized by Islam.

The Boston Marathon is a regular annual event held on Patriots' Day to honor the anniversary of the American Revolutionary Battles of Lexington and Concord on April 19, 1775.

These were the first battles of the American Revolutionary War. The day is observed publicly but, though the law encourages people to celebrate it, it is not treated as a public holiday. Re-enactments of the first battles of the Revolution are conducted in Lexington at the Green, and at The Old North Bridge in Concord, Massachusetts.

In the morning, mounted Revolutionary soldiers with state police escorts retrace the rides of Paul Revere, calling out warnings that "the British are coming", "the British are coming".

This sad story recounts how two young boys came to this country from the old world with their parents to apply for asylum in the United States because of religious persecution in their home country, Chechnya, which was under Russian rule.

They were accepted in America, the home of immigrants, where all are welcome regardless of race, color, or religious creed and where opportunity to achieve any dream is available and open to all with the energy to work hard in this wonderful world of freedom and opportunity.

The boys were well accepted in their communities as they grew to manhood participating and achieving excellence in their local public schools athletic activities and gaining admirers from their peers. They were good students and generally well-regarded. They were said to be "nice guys" and enjoyed all the opportunities afforded them, including something very new to them, dates with American girls. The older boy even married an American girl and fathered a baby.

Though they came to this country having been raised in the Islamic faith, it does not appear that they had radical tendencies until they were influenced by one or more members of their mosque in America who have been reported as having "radicalized them".

They also became expert computer users and frequently used this medium to search around the world for what turned out to be radical information about the Islamic objective to take over the world. As young boys will be, they were influenced by romantic ideals without considering the fundamental evil of these ideas. They were thoroughly brainwashed and indoctrinated by their religion. Their religious fervor overcame their intellectual sensibilities and permitted them to conduct this incident of monumental horror to an innocent audience of women and children.

They worked with great secrecy as close friends and associates said they had no knowledge of what went on in the boy's heads. Even their school roommates had no clue according to what was reported. The older of the two was said to have visited Russia prior to the bombing and may have been trained in terrorist's activities during the six months of his visit.

This is a story of how relatively innocent minds can be influenced and brainwashed by evil ideas in the name of a dominating religion. It tells the tale of how two apparently innocent young boys were made into killers to achieve the objectives of an international violent theocracy called Islam.

PREAMBLE

"Terrorists! They call us terrorists! They are the dirty terrorists—every time they send a drone over there to Afghanistan and Pakistan to kill innocent people. That's real terrorism; they are experts at it, Omar."

"Yes, but didn't we start it first with all the suicide bombings?" Asked Omar.

"Who cares who was first," Mohammed replied, "Obama says he'll never go to war with Islam, but isn't every drone they send over there killing women and children an act of war?"

"Mohammed, it's got to stop someplace," pleaded Omar.

"It will never stop until we dominate them. That's what the Imam says. Kill them. Kill them. Kill every one of them: all of the infidels and especially all of the Jews. I dedicate my life to this," said Mohammed.

CHAPTER 1

THE NEW WORLD

"We could never count on a peaceful life in our home country. From my earliest memory, there were soldiers from Russia burning our houses and killing our people. First, under Putin: then my father told us of the violence under Stalin when thousands of our people were massacred simply because we were followers of Islam. And grandfather before him spoke of the pogroms under the Tsar because we were a Muslim people under the Russian rulers who followed Orthodox Christianity. Though my father and mother had four children, an older brother and sister were killed in the last purge. My younger brother Omar and I are the only remaining children in our family.

My father determined that Chechnya was so violent; he decided to immigrate to the United States, looking for a better, freer life for his family, so he and my mother with my brother and I boarded a ship on the Baltic bound for the new world.

I had never been on an ocean going ship before this experience. It was also especially new moving our home which was kind of a traumatic experience. We had one small stateroom for the whole family on the ship. There was one washbasin all of us had to use, but no toilet. It was down a hall, shared with other families. There was one shower there also but it smelled pretty bad.

If you think taking an ocean voyages is fun, think again. Our small room was so crowded with four of us; we spent all of our time, except sleeping, in the great main room where we also took our meals. The sea was rough and stormy so the boat bounced around a lot that made us sick and the food really was not that appealing, but we had nothing to do but to put up with it.

We ended up in New York. My father applied for asylum claiming religious persecution in the old country. We were accepted and lived there on what they call the lower East side for a short time.

There, we lived a life crowded into tenements with other freedom seekers, immigrants from all over the world, but no one seemed to mind as we all were looking for the American dream of opportunity to raise one's family in peace, where life, opportunity, and freedom for all is respected, regardless of who you are, what you believed, or where you came from.

I must admit that the idea of freedom was really new to me. Since our whole lives were spent in Chechnya and in a Muslim world, really freedom was dependent upon whether Allah granted it or not. So I'm a little confused about what freedom really means as certainly, under Islam freedom is defined by the Koran and the only freedom that we have is that which is granted by Allah.

We had been accustomed to better living conditions at home but father promised us we'd soon move on to a better situation. Soon, we were invited to go to my uncle's house in New Jersey. He was my father's brother who had lived in the US almost 20 years and had become much Americanized.

That was certainly the happiest time of my life.

Living in America is something I never could have visualized. I had heard so many bad things about it from my mosque and the government at home but really none of it is true. The people here are friendly, free, and smart and they actually live without locking the doors of their homes. My uncle, Charlie, my dad's brother, just loves it here and is helping us get adjusted. It didn't take long though. We've only been here a few years so far and already I'm beginning to feel like an American, enjoying the kind of freedoms I never dreamed were possible in Chechnya. I even got part-time work so I could buy a car, something I could never have afforded in

Chechnya. I even started going out with some girls. I had never done that before, either.

That's something that is pretty amazing too. American girls are just nothing like they are in Chechnya. Here, they do everything a boy does and are treated like equals. And they even drive cars and go out alone. At home, a male relative has to go out with them otherwise they can't leave the home. But not here! I'm not sure I totally like it but girls are girls and they sure are fun. Even Omar is beginning to have dates, as they call it here.

There are so many places to go with a date. Both Omar and I have learned to dance and that is really a blast. We could never do that at home. Music and dancing is not permitted under Islam. I guess I'm really becoming an American. Not so bad: except I wish they would look better on Islam, which they don't. I'm not quite sure why.

Our mother made sure that we went to mosque every day for prayers. We were absolutely required to follow this routine. At the mosque, we studied the Quran and listened to the Imam tell us about the future of Islam in the United States. It really came down to this: Islam is destined to rule the world and the objective right now is that we eventually will take over the United States. I'm not sure if I really go along with this but I don't think I really have much choice. As I read the Quran and learn more about sharia law, I wonder how that's going to fit in with what they call freedom here in the US. I guess I have a lot to learn.

But, America is certainly the land of opportunity and riches. Omar was 6 years old when we arrived at uncle Charlie's in New Jersey and I was 12 when we went to live there. We enrolled in the local public schools and quickly learned English under the friendly and welcoming teachers in the land we almost began to feel was our own. But we did miss many of the traditions of our homeland where our religion, Islam, was very important to the majority of the population, as it was to us. However, daily prayers at our local mosque were required and we happily attended. Actually, I was surprised that there were so many people who believed in Islam in America. Most of us Muslims got along like everybody else as far as I knew though there was some prejudice in the air.

3

Many Muslims were just trying to be Americans but some were not. They seemed to want to keep the old world ideas and be Muslims first and Americans second. Religion was more important than citizenship to many of them. I keep balancing back and forth on the subject. Most of the time I feel I want to be a good American but to be so I have to give up a lot of Muslim ideas and I just don't know whether I'm can do that or not.

The most important is sharia law compared to what the Americans call their Constitution. To be a true American we're supposed to follow the Constitution but in order to be a true Muslim we must follow the Koran and sharia law and there are differences. It's a difficult problem for all devoted Muslims. What is more important, man's laws, or Allah's laws? Good Muslims must follow Allah.

Really, as Muslims we look upon Allah as being the final word on what we should do and how we should act. And our Imam tells us what Allah wants us to do. It all seemed very simple back in Chechnya where everyone knew what they should do. Over here there's a lot of confusion at least in my mind about what's right. But really when you get right down to it, you simply have to follow the Constitution or you're not an American. We read a lot about the Constitution in school as well as the Declaration of Independence and the Bill of Rights. All of these documents talk about a kind of freedom that really most Muslims don't completely understand. We just never had it. I guess, as Muslims, we really don't feel that freedom is as important as what the Imam tells us is right. And what the Koran teaches.

Our uncle Charlie, a name he adapted to be more Americanized, worked in a local machine parts factory where he had attained a management position and made a wonderful living which provided for us all as we were getting adjusted to the new country which presented some challenges because they did many things differently than we did at home. Uncle Charlie told us that he had given up being a Muslim when he came to the new country and he felt fine about that. I always thought it was something that was pretty bad but Uncle Charlie says it seems to be working out okay for him. He doesn't go to church or mosque at all. That would really scare me. My religion has always been very important to me. My mother and brother feel as I do: dad, less so.

"Years ago," Uncle Charlie explained, "when I first arrived and after I learned to read and write in English, I discovered a book by Robert Green Ingersoll, his autobiography," Uncle Charlie went on.

"It really opened my eyes to ideas I had never thought about before. Ingersoll talks a lot about freethinking. He spoke about the freedom that comes from independent thinking, doing away with dogma and demanding evidence. Ingersoll was a lawyer and legislator and most noted as an orator, the most popular of the age, when oratory was public entertainment. He spoke on every subject, from slavery to Voltaire, Shakespeare to Reconstruction, but his most popular subjects were atheism and the sanctity and the importance of logic and reason. In a lecture entitled "The Great Infidels," he attacked the religious doctrine of Hell: "All the meanness, all the revenge, all the selfishness, all the cruelty, all the hatred, all the infamy of which the heart of man is capable, grew, blossomed, and bore fruit in this one word—Hell." He said it was a damnable idea.

Uncle Charlie went on, "Ingersoll said that in a God who would believe that his people would go to hell, under any circumstances, was not a very sensible God. Besides, it was illogical to believe in God."

"Here's a quote from Epicurus from 270 BC: Quotation on the logic of the existence of God:

"Is God willing to prevent evil, but not able? Then he is not omnipotent. Is he able, but not willing? Then he is malevolent. Is he both able and willing? Then: whence cometh evil? Is he neither able nor willing? Then why call him God?"

"What does that mean exactly? Well, I'm hoping to dissect it piece by piece and let "believers" try to come up with some kind of rebuttal. Unfortunately this will not be easy, as this quote takes care of about 99% of "faith" based arguments."

"Is God willing to prevent evil, but not able? Then he is not omnipotent."

"For the first part of the quote he is saying:" Would God prevent evil if he could, but not able to? Then he is not an all-powerful being, or God."

"The next part of the quote is more of what Christians believe God is even without realizing it.

Is he able, but not willing? Then he is malevolent."

"Is he able to stop evil, but doesn't want to? Then he is evil."

"This is a great one for Christians who say he can stop it, and he would if he could:

"Is he both able and willing, then: whence cometh evil?"

"Is he able to stop evil and would if he could? Then where does hell and evil come from?"

"My favorite final piece, is: "Is he neither able nor willing? Then why call him God?"

"Can he not stop evil and doesn't care? Then why call him God?"

"Can anyone prove Epicurus wrong? No matter what God you choose, either evil or powerful, it's not something I would ever pray to or devote my entire life to." Uncle Charlie was very convincing.

Uncle Charlie found Ingersoll "inspirational," he said. His writings were very important in his becoming a free thinker and giving up the ancient superstitions of Islam as they are without reason and without evidence", he said.

Uncle Charlie had become an atheist, which was what Karl Marx was. I guess atheism is getting more popular in the United States like it is in much of Russia.

I guess the biggest difference I found in America was that most of our friends didn't go to church even though many said they were Christians.

Some were even Jews. I had never known a Jew before. But they are like everybody else, aren't they? But even though they didn't go to church, they still, mostly were believers, they say, in their religion's history. I found that most of the Jews that I met were really atheists, though cultural Jews.

When our American friends found out that we went to the mosque every day to pray, they were amazed and even made fun of us. But the mosque was an important part of our life. It was something that we could never give up. Daily worship and prayers were essential to our day as Muslims. Our Imam told us that if we didn't attend mosque daily that we would really get into big trouble. We didn't want that. And Islam imposed the threat of death to anyone who left the faith. So there was no alternative.

Soon after we arrived in the United States, the World Trade Center in New York was bombed on 9/11 with the loss of thousands of American lives. Muslims were blamed for that though I have been told later by our Imam that this was really a CIA plot just to place the blame on our people. Nonetheless, it made life difficult for us as Muslims.

I was in high school and Omar in grade school. One of the most exciting things that became available to us was the computer. It's like magic. All you do is press a button and you can get information on practically anything. We were taught how to use it in school so both Omar and I soon became very knowledgeable about this new technology which neither of us had ever heard about before we came to America.

The other amazing product was the cell phone. I guess I had heard about it but nobody we knew had one in Chechnya, at least where we lived. It's so tiny you can put it in a shirt pocket and you can call people all over the world just by pressing a button or two. America really is an amazing place with all these new technical developments. I don't know why we don't have them in our country . . . . I mean Chechnya.

Another thing that was really wonderful was the ability to tap into a lot of the things going on around the world with the computer. I began investigating things in Russia and was really astonished at what was happening there even though when I lived in Russia I never heard about those things. Right now there is another purge going on for the region around Chechnya. These are Russians again killing off my people. I'm sure glad I'm here where it's safe, Mohammed thought.

I remember the course on the computer that I was taking in high school was more advanced than the one that Omar had in grade school. But he and I often worked together in the evening accessing all kinds of information. Omar was really getting good at it . . . . maybe even better than I was in some ways.

"Mohammed, how do you get this thing to print out," Omar asked?

"It's real easy, Omar. See this key: this is the one you press but first you have to have a document up on the screen. You know what a document is?"

"Oh, sure," Omar answered.

"Then when you press this button and the printer automatically prints it out. Wonderful isn't it?"

"Can I do the same thing on my computer," Mohammed?

"No, Omar, you have to be hooked up with a printer like I have. When you get a little older, I can get you a printer too. Now let me show you how you can make your image on the screen any size you want."

"Oh no, Mohammed, I know how to do that. All you do is hit this button that asks you how big you want the font. See? I learned that in school."

"You're really learning," replied Mohammed.

The computer became one of the most important items in their life and they both became very expert in its use, something that later on was going to provide them with information that was to contribute to the kind of people they became.

CHAPTER 2

PARENTS RETURN TO CHECHNYA

Our mother got into some kind of trouble with the police. She was questioned by what they call the CIA and then released. She wouldn't talk about it.

Then one day the phone rang and asked for Mr. Tarrkahn. "Hey, pop, you're wanted on the phone."

"Hello, this is Mr. Tarrkahn."

"This is Officer Adams at the police department. Here is Mrs. Tarrkahn. She wants to talk to you."

"This is all a mistake. This is all a mistake," mother cried, "but they're holding me here and you have to come to get me out," she exclaimed.

"Oh, praise Allah what is wrong?" Dad asked nervously.

"Just come and get me and I'll tell you everything," she answered.

He drove to the police station where she was in a compound. The officer explained that she had been apprehended shoplifting by a store security officer.

"It wasn't that. It wasn't bad at all. I put a fountain pen in my purse and intended to pay for it and then forgot when I went out the door a security officer grabbed me and called the police. It's all a mistake," my mother explained.

"Anyway Mr. Tarrkahn," the officer explained, "The bond for release is $500 until a court hearing." The bond was paid and they drove home.

During those early years our mother and father said they were so lonely for Chechnya and their old friends and family, and motivated by the police incident they eventually decided to return to Chechnya where my father managed to get a very good administrative job in the government. It was sad to see them depart.

My brother and I were getting into our teens when we learned about a region that was called New England. It sounded very attractive and with excellent schools, so we both decided to move to the Boston area. Our uncle Charlie helped us with the early finances for which we are so grateful.

Then we found out about government assistance. Unbelievably, both Omar and I managed to get signed up for regular money for education from the US government so with that plus the money we were earning by part-time work, we really could live very well while we went to school. I even traded my car for a newer Mercedes that was in amazingly good shape. America is really fantastic. It takes care of everybody.

Both Omar and I loved athletics so we both got involved in high school sports. Boxing and wrestling was my sport. Omar was best at running and basketball. The Boston area was just crazy about all sports and frequently conducted big public events like the Boston Marathon that drew runners from all over the world. Omar entered it one year.

I got very involved in boxing and won the Golden gloves heavyweight championship two times for New England. But I was barred from the national tournament of champions because I was not a United States citizen, even though Omar was. That really hurt because I had worked so hard to be a champion boxer. But I'm beginning to wonder if I really want to be a US citizen. I keep finding out things over here that I don't like too well.

The free and easy girls are one thing the other is their attitude towards Islam. Islam is number one in my mind. Anyone who doesn't believe in it is really, as we say, an infidel, and according to the Quran must be either given diminished status or killed. That's what the book says and also what I hear from my Imam. Yeah, America has a lot to learn and I would like to help show them the way.

We always regularly went to the mosque for prayers daily. The Imam preached a lot about how superior Islam was to any of the religions in the United States and even the rest of the world.

Being the younger brother, Omar mostly followed my lead which I was happy to provide. In some ways I was almost a father to him because I was six years older. I can remember one subject that continues to really puzzle him and that was how you treat girls. His big question to me was, "Mohammed, there are girls in all my classes and they treat them the same just like they are boys. How come they do that?"

Well Omar, it's a completely different world in America and we are just going to have to get used to it until Islam takes over. In some ways it's kind of nice, but not moral. Since the girls go to school here, they get much smarter than at home, don't you think? I must admit, I kinda like this aspect of America. But on balance, I think America would be better with Islam being very strong.

"Yes, but they talk back to you like they are equal," said Omar.

They are equal here in the United States. That's the way things are here. Though I agree with you, it's hard to get used to. I prefer the way we regard girls back home. They should keep the house and make babies and do what they're told.

One of the things I really liked about the United States was the availability of good-looking clothes. I especially liked white fur and snakeskin. So my friends call me pretty flamboyant in the way I dress sometimes. But I like to dress up. I could never do that at home. Yeah, things are different here.

"I have been dating a girl and have asked her out to have a Coke with me. Her name is Eleanor and she's from a little town somewhere near which they call, The Cape. I'll have to introduce you to her. I met her at my school. She's a Christian-a Catholic, so that's a problem but I think that can be solved. Her father is a doctor," Mohammed said.

I went down there last weekend to see her. We had a good time swimming in the ocean but you should see the bathing suit see wore or maybe I should say the bathing suit she didn't wear. Girls do things in this country that would be against the law where we come from.

"You want to meet my parents," she asked.

"Sure", I answered. "Is your house far from here?"

"No, only a few miles"

So we go over. It was a Sunday so her mother and father were home. We all sat in the living room while I got the going over with questions that didn't set too well with them when I answered that I was a Muslim. Since they were Catholic, we really had nothing when it comes to religion in common. I guess they were pretty strict about it. But then I am too, about my religion. Certainly, if I was to get serious about Eleanor, she would have to become a Muslim. That's absolute. I suppose it would be the same the other way around.

Her parents were polite but that's about all. I made some excuse about getting back to school and that was that. I really never saw them again as Eleanor told me they were not very happy about the fact that I was a Muslim and really forbid her to see me anymore. But we didn't pay any attention to that and went right on dating anyway.

We all talk a lot about getting along in the world, and it sounds like a good idea but it will never happen until Islam takes over. Everyone has to follow Islam because it's the right thing to do. That's what my Imam says. And I know we will succeed even if it takes 1000 years.

Allah is great.

CHAPTER 3

GROWING UP IN BOSTON

We had rented a room near the high school that Omar attended. I started at one of the local night-school colleges studying mechanical drawing, so I had to use the bus to get to school. I could never find parking for my car. I even got the government to pay most of my college costs. This country is so rich. It's really amazing.

Omar got very involved in running and I continued in boxing. I was really beginning to make a name for myself around the community and I must admit I liked it. I also spent a lot of time working on my classical music which I really love. Though I'm getting pretty good with a violin, I really prefer the piano. I'm singing along with the piano and even have thought about joining a local musicians group just to play around town, though I really like classical music on the piano the best. That is the most fun.

"You know, Mohammed, the government says it's OK to take up a musical instrument," said Omar. "You seem to enjoy it so much and it goes over just great at any parties we go to. At home we couldn't do that."

"No, Islam doesn't allow music," Mohammed added, "but we really have to follow Islam, no matter what." But while we're here, we can do what we want.

We really didn't seem to get along too well with our schoolmates or our neighbors. They simply regarded us as different because we attended a mosque each day to say our prayers: which was kind of looked down upon by most people. Also when they found out that we are Muslims, they kept asking us about the bombing of the trade Center in New York and why we did it. It made me kind of mad. We didn't do it. It was just a bunch of radical terrorists or maybe a CIA plot. That's what our Imam says.

The Boston mosque that we attended was a lot stricter than the one in New Jersey near our uncle's house. The Boston Imam spent most of his time talking about how terrible it is that Americans are making war on Islamic countries in the Middle East. I really agree with him. What right has the US got to go over there and tell us what to do? I mean Muslims. Muslims want their own country and will have it. I feel it coming. We will make it happen.

I met someone at the mosque who was an older man who called himself Bosni and had a big black beard that flowed down to his big belly. He spent a lot of time talking to me about how lucky we were to be followers of Islam and how Americans just didn't understand our religion. He really knew a lot about Islam and I was impressed. He also told me he's studying to be an Imam. Wouldn't that be something? An Imam is the guy that runs the mosque—kind of like the main preacher. I don't think I'd like being an Imam. It takes a lot of school and I'm getting a little tired of school.

"America doesn't understand Islam, but someday it will when we take over," said Bosni. "Islam has been around much longer than America. God willing, Islam will take over the world, it just takes time and we have all the time in the world."

"You know, Omar," Mohammed said, "I never gave an awful lot of thought about what Islam really teaches until I started talking often to Bosni. I'm really finding out what the true intent is. And you know it's all in the Koran. The object is really to take over the world and make it all Islam. Wouldn't that be neat? Then we'd really have a peaceful world. There would be no wars because Islam would not permit it".

But first we have to get stronger particularly in the United States. That means numbers; we just need a larger population of Muslims. Our Boston mosque Imam in his last sermon talked about no Muslim should be converted to another faith. He said, "What should be done to a Muslim who converts to another faith? "We kill him," he says, "kill him, kill,

kill . . . You have to kill him, you understand? And then adulterers and homosexuals are to be singled out for death. "Adulterers, he says, are to be stoned to death—and as for homosexuals, and women who "make themselves like a man, a woman like a man . . . the punishment is kill, kill them, throw them from the highest place. "These punishments, the preacher says, are to be implemented in a future Islamic state."

"Bosni has even convinced me to give up boxing and music which I love, but really Islam comes first and music isn't allowed under Islam, neither is dancing. If we're going to be good Muslims, and be moral, we will just have to lead a different kind of life than the way we've been living here in America," Mohammed added.

Here's what Ayatollah Khamenei said "Those who know nothing about Islam pretend that Islam counsels against war. Those people are witless. Islam says: 'Kill all the unbelievers just as they would kill you all!' Does this mean that Muslims should sit back until they are devoured by the infidel? Islam says: 'Kill them, put them to the sword and scatter them.' Islam says: 'Whatever good there is exists thanks to the sword.' The sword is the key to Paradise, which can be opened only for the Holy Warriors! Does all this mean that Islam is a religion that prevents men from waging war? I spit upon those foolish souls who make such a claim."

"In the Muslim community, the holy war is a religious duty, because of the universalism of the Muslim mission and the obligation to convert everybody to Islam either by persuasion or force. The other religious groups Christianity and Judaism did not have a universal mission, and the holy war was not a religious duty to them, save only for purposes of defense. "Islam makes it incumbent on all adult males to prepare themselves for the conquest of countries so that the writ of Islam is obeyed in every country in the world."

"The big thing I'm learning from Bosni is Americans are waging a lot of wars against our people in the Middle East and that's not right. Bosni showed me websites that prove that the CIA was behind the Trade Center terrorist attacks of September 11 and Jews control the world. I really hate Jews. That's what the Koran tells me. Jews are really pigs and dogs, according to the Quran. But I keep meeting Jews in the United States that aren't bad at all. I'm confused."

"You know those Israeli Jews are really raising a lot of hell. They're lobbing missiles into Palestine and taking over land that should not be theirs," Omar said.

"Bosni told me the other day, that what is going on in our mosque in Boston is going on all over the United States. They're trying to teach all Muslims who go to mosques in this country and learn exactly what is the truth about Islam and what our real aim is, to take over the world. And we will do it, according to Bosni," Mohammed emphasized.

"You know we almost did that a few hundred years ago when we took over Spain and Italy and a lot of southern France all the way up to Vienna in Austria," said Mohammad, "and that's what Bosni told me. Now he says we have all this money from oil, he says, and we're on our way to doing it right this time. And, we'll succeed. Allah is great."

Early on, Bosni came over to our room to talk about the real Islam and we had long discussions about what Islam was all about and how it was so important that we keep up on our religion here in this country where Islam was not looked upon in much favor. In fact, I think most of the people that I met really felt that Islam was very threatening after they bombed the World Trade Center especially. At least that is what everybody said. I know at the mosque with my new friend, Bosni that we really learned that the whole business of 9/11 in New York was a CIA plot.

Bosni also said, "the religion of Islam should be above all, so that all areas of life could be guided by Islam, and so that the earth could be cleansed from unbelief" "The foremost duty of Islam is to depose the government and society of unbelievers (jahiliyyah) from the leadership of man." (Sayyid Qutb, Egyptian) "Uniting the five pillars of Islam is the principle Jihad (lit. struggle). In Islam a Muslim must struggle against himself and his habits to submit fully to God. He must also struggle to guide his family, relatives, and friends to bring them to Islam and to convey the message of Islam itself. Since Islam is totalistic, Muslims wherever they may be, must struggle and sacrifice their energy, time, and material resources to establish Muslim congregations, mosques, madrassas (religious schools) for the maintenance and spread of Islam. Where Muslims make up a substantial fraction of the population, they must struggle to establish the Islamic Shari'ah (law) as their rule for living, with the aim to ultimately establish a full Islamic state in which Islam would be the ruling ideology and system. To understand this last point is very important for it is part and parcel of Islam to seek its full manifestation and where Muslims fail politically or economically, they also fail spiritually. It is innate to Islam to be militantly uncompromising with alien systems since all sovereignty and glory belongs to God, to the Prophets (PBUH) and to the believers." Suicide bombers openly call themselves terrorists with pride since the Koran calls for Muslims to act as terrorists in Koran 8:12. "I will instill terror into the hearts of the unbelievers: smite ye above their necks and smite all their finger-tips off them".

One of the things that Bosni always kept talking about was the immorality in this country of the US. Women who walk around half dressed and go out by themselves, even driving their own cars. And how couples sleep together before they are married and even some of the married couples cheat and there is no law against it. Also everyone drinks alcohol and suggestive music is played practically every place. In some ways it's kind of fun but Bosni says it's against the religion of Islam. And I have to follow the religion. There is no choice. If you don't do what the Imam says, the punishment is pretty severe. They could even kill you.

Bosni says it's just a matter of time before Islam is able to take over much of the Western world for many reasons. The most important is that we really believe in what we're doing, whereas most of the population, in these countries, has no real objective. We also have bigger families so our numbers are steadily increasing as a percentage of the total population like in England. We will outnumber everybody before too long. Bosni says maybe 20 or 30 years at the most. I wouldn't be surprised. I guess they really can't wait for that. When the whole world is under Islam, then we will have real peace, like the Koran says.

Bosni says, "American troops in Afghanistan and Iraq and Pakistan cannot be allowed. Those are countries for followers of Islam not for infidels, which are what the Americans are."

"But we have a plan for America. It's called infiltration and they don't even know about it. Most people in this country don't care and that's the way you want to keep them ignorant to the facts."

"One of the most amazing things is the fact that even the United States president is talking like he is under Islam philosophy. We certainly know he was born in an Islamist family according to the history that is available. There is a book out on the subject of Obama being a follower of Islam. It wouldn't surprise me," added Bosni.

Bosni was very important in influencing the changing of the mindset of the two boys. As an older man, also, they respected him and almost venerated him. It was almost as if he had cast some kind of a spell over them. This influence, along with the information they were able to get from their computer slowly changed their positions as they were becoming thoroughly indoctrinated in the Islamic philosophy.

Omar had been doing a lot of running and even decided to join the Boston marathon one year. He didn't do very well in the race. In any event, it seems like the blacks from Africa are the best runners. "I don't know why they even allow blacks in events like that", said Omar. They sure wouldn't where we came from. Blacks really aren't that smart. All you have to do is look at most of Africa and they are still ignorant peasants. But everyone here in America talks about equality. I'm not so sure I believe in that. Some people are just better than others. They even say that women are equal to men, which is pretty crazy as far as I'm concerned. Women should stay in the home and raise babies and keep the house clean and do the cooking.

I spent a lot of my time on the wrestling team and managed to develop some pretty big muscles that impressed the girls. That wasn't too bad. But I still was amazed how all the girls acted so independently like they knew what they were doing. That was one of the hard things to get used to but also a lot of them are really sexy. That's something I could get used to real easy. I'm glad my mom and pop are back in Russia. Especially, mom wouldn't put up with it but then she's a woman.

I guess our time really revolved pretty much around the mosque and the computer. We really didn't socialize a lot. One of the imams was pretty actively preaching about how someday Islam is going to take over the world. I think that would be pretty cool and I even think maybe I should get involved in something like that. I discussed that with Omar and though he wasn't so sure but he said he would go along with whatever I did.

"Mohammed," Omar asked, "what makes everyone talk so bad about Islam?"

That seemed to bother Omar a lot. "Well," I answered, "remember there were over 3000 people killed on 9/11," I explained, "and everyone says it was Muslims who did it. That's the first thing"

"But Bosni says it's was a CIA plot," said Omar. "I really don't know what to believe."

"Just be sure you believe Bosni, Omar, as he knows what's right. I'm just convinced of that. Especially his showing me how living under Islam is so much more moral than Christianity. I like that. Women just shouldn't be allowed to be like they are here, running around half naked and feeling like they are equal to men."

We kept going to school and even increasing our association with girls. That would sound strange to anybody at home, but that's the way it is. In fact I'm getting very serious about Eleanor I might even ask her to marry me. But of course she would have to convert to Islam; otherwise I couldn't possibly even think about marrying her. Her dad really doesn't like me very much and has been trying to discourage Eleanor but she likes me and that's what matters. I think she might make a pretty good wife.

"Mohammed, do you really think you could marry somebody that wasn't from our religion?" asked Omar, "even if she agrees to convert to Islam?"

Well, we'll see. We'll see.

CHAPTER 4

WATCHING THE WORLD SCENE

"Did you see the paper this morning, Mohammed? It's all about how the Americans are taking over Afghanistan like they did Iraq. That's not right, I think. Afghanistan is for Afghanistan's, not Americans, the same with Iraq," Omar said. "I really hate their taking over other countries and I hate them, too."

"I sure agree with you on that subject but what in the world can we do about it," Omar?

"I was watching on television last night and it really is a sad subject. The Americans should get out of there and leave Afghanistan for their people, Afghanistan is for Afghanistan's" replied Mohammed.

"I certainly fully agree. It makes me just mad as hell, when I see foreigners in Islamic countries trying to take over. Bosni told me last night that is one more example of how the Americans are trying to take over the Middle East and colonize it like the British did not too many years ago," said Omar.

"Mohammed, do you ever think it would be good for us to go over there and help?" asked Omar.

"No, Omar, at least not right now. We have our education to finish and then maybe we can do that. Besides I like the free money from the government and driving around in my Mercedes. We couldn't do that at home. Meanwhile I'm also making good money at my job even though it's part-time. I may ask Eleanor to marry me. Besides, probably we can help more by staying here," replied Mohammed. Bosni says, there are lots we can do.

"Boy that is a big decision, Mohammed, do you think she will? I mean marry you" asked Omar.

"Well I'm going to ask Eleanor tonight but only if she's willing to convert to Islam. That's required," said Mohammad.

Eleanor Adams was raised in an upper-middle-class family in Rhode Island. Her father was a doctor and she was someone with a good record in high school growing up normally in a privileged environment. She decided to enroll at Suffolk University in Boston, where she was known as a social butterfly and free-spirited. That's where she met Mohammad.

Friends introduced her to Mohammed known for his big muscles and flashy clothing. Her life began to change as she became more religious; becoming obsessed with him and eventually she converted to Islam. She married him and had a daughter dropping out of college and moving into his rundown apartment in Cambridge after living a life in an upper-class neighborhood in comfortable surroundings. She now found herself on relief living a very low class life.

Eleanor and Mohammed met for a hamburger at McDonald's when he popped the question with the admonition that she must convert. She was happy about the proposal as she was infatuated with Mohammed, but wondered about the conversion. "Eleanor, you really don't have any choice. It's converting to Islam or else no marriage. That's a requirement of Islam." Mohammed was very sure of himself on this.

"I don't know, Mohammed, my family are all devout Catholics and that's the way I was raised. I just don't know what to do," Eleanor replied.

"Well, Eleanor, I don't have any choice as it is the law of our religion that we cannot marry anyone unless they are willing to convert. And remember our religion comes first, darling," added Mohammed.

"Well what about our children?" asked Eleanor.

"Of course, they would have to be raised as good Muslims following Islam too. There just is no other way." Mohammed was really asserting himself as he has not done so before this. But he felt very confident in what he was saying.

It took a while over a period of weeks but Eleanor finally agreed, much to the regrets of her family. They had a small ceremony at the local mosque. Eleanor's parents wouldn't even attend so only their friends were there. Now, she also was required to change her clothing to black with a head covering. She finally went to a full burqa. At first it was difficult but the relationship was so strong that she managed it. Now, after it's all over she's known throughout the world as the widow of the Boston bomber and being investigated to see to what extent she was involved in the bombing. Her life has been substantially changed for the worse.

Mohammed kept up his regular meetings at the mosque with his brother, Omar, always joining him.

The Imam was an inspired speaker. He talked a lot about the peacefulness of Islam and that infidels either must convert to Islam or be killed. That's directly from the Koran. He made it sound easy . . . . like the natural thing to do.

"Some people say that Islam is violent but all you have to do is read the Quran to find it's very peaceful and loving. Just wait when we take over the world and everyone is Islam—then we will have a peaceful world," said the Imam. That was always the main emphasis of his preaching and both Mohammed and Omar fully believed what he said.

The principal subjects mainly discussed at the mosque by the local Imam were the wars in the Middle East. By that time, Saddam Hussein in Iraq had been killed and Afghanistan was at the height of their war and pretty much losing it. This was always a major problem with all followers of Islam.

CHAPTER 5

TRAVEL TO RUSSIA

"Hey, Omar, I just got a wonderful offer."

"What was that, Mohammed?"

"Bosni says Islam needs people to help them in their international work. I would have to go to Russia to get some training. It sounds pretty exciting especially since I really want to help Islam reach their objectives of expansion throughout the world and conversion of infidels."

"How long do you think you would be gone, Mohammed?"

"I don't know exactly, Omar, but at least a few months according to Bosni. Do you think I should do it?"

"Well, Mohammed it is really up to you but it sounds like a good opportunity to get ahead and serve Allah. I'm still busy in school but I think I can get along."

"I'll help you out, Omar, as I have some extra money from my job."

So Bosni made the arrangements for Mohammed who went back to Russia where he stayed off and on with his father. His mother was divorced from his father by this time. Mohammed enrolled in the training program described by Bosni.

It was pretty rigorous but Mohammed was in excellent condition so all the physical training didn't bother him at all. He also learned about bomb making and handling various kinds of firearms which was all new to him.

He really enjoyed it though and it gave him a feeling of belonging to something that was bigger than he was.

The leaders were all pretty tough guys dedicated to the job of making Islam number one in the world. They talked about it endlessly. It was really almost a second religion to them. They stressed the idea that was basic in all of the Islamic writings that all infidels had to be converted or be killed. This was written repeatedly in the Quran.

The program was seven days a week and involved living outside in the elements so everybody got toughened up. Mohammed's father knew what Mohammed was doing and fully supported him.

They also spent a few hours every day in the intense study of the Quran and a complete understanding of sharia law so essential to Islam. They were required to memorize the Koran which took a lot of time but Mohammed managed to recite much of it by memory.

Sharia law is also known as Islamic law covers, generally, the following points to be carefully followed by all good Muslims who believe in Islam:

Here is a partial list of the basic tenants of Islamic (Sharia) Law:

- A man may marry up to four wives but a woman may only have one husband.
- A man may divorce a woman by repeating three times, "I divorce you."
- In court proceedings woman's testimony is only considered half that of a man.
- A woman's inheritance is only half that of a man's.
- Theft is punished by amputation of hands and/or heads.
- Adultery by women is punished by stoning her to death.
- Homosexuality and sodomy are punishable by death.
- Men may marry anyone of any faith who must convert to Islam.
- Women may only marry men of Islam faith.
- Apostasy (leaving Islam) is punishable by death.
- All infidels (those who are not Muslims) are to be killed.
- All Jews are to be killed.

- A father must kill a daughter who was raped as she has soiled family honor.
- Young women must be circumcised, (This has been called, female genital mutilation.)

Author's Note: Female genital mutilation (FGM), also known as female genital cutting (FGC) and female circumcision (FC), is defined by the World Health Organization (WHO) as "all procedures that involve partial or total removal of the external female genitalia, or other injury to the female genital organs for non-medical reasons." According to WHO, it is practiced mainly in 28 countries in western, eastern, and north-eastern Africa, and in parts of Asia and the Middle East. The organization estimates that 140 million women and girls around the world have experienced the procedure, including 101 million in Africa. Female genital mutilation is believed to have originated in the Pharaonic period amongst Afro-Asiatic (Hamito-Semitic) communities inhabiting the Red Sea area, from where it later spread to other regions. The procedure is typically carried out on girls from a few days old to puberty. The surgery may take place in a hospital, but is usually performed, without anesthesia, by a traditional circumciser using a knife, razor or scissors. There have been efforts by international bodies since 1979 to end the practice, and in 2012 the United Nations General Assembly unanimously passed a resolution banning it but it is secretly practiced still by some Muslims in the United States.

Mohammed, in Russia, had a little trouble in the beginning with the language problem. He'd gotten rusty living in the United States but he was soon conversing like a native and loving it.

One of his instructors named Ben Allie became very friendly. He asked Mohammed how he liked living in the United States.

"Oh I guess it's okay, Ben Allie. It has its good points and its bad ones. The biggest problem is most of the people don't follow Islam. I know because whenever they found out that I was a Muslim, they kind of turned me off. But I didn't care. I'm working on something much bigger which we all know," Mohammed replied.

"Well, that is something we are going to change, Mohammed. That's why you're here in training. We've got a lot of people in Washington high up in the government so the job should get easier as we go along in the states," Ben Allie replied.

"Have you ever thought of moving to the United States, Ben Allie?" asked Mohammed.

"Well I thought about it but right now I got a good job training people right here. It doesn't pay very much but it's very satisfying and it brings me a lot of respect from the local people," replied Ben Allie.

"Yes, I can see what you mean, Ben Allie. I wouldn't mind doing it myself."

"No, don't talk like that. You could get in trouble. We want to train you so you can get back to the United States and get some projects going. And one of the most important is setting up some bomb sites where we can terrorize civilians and get them to realize that Islam is important and will be taking over the world. I know you can do it. I'm counting on you and so are our comrades," said Ben Allie.

"Well, I'll do the best I can. I really believe in this whole thing. I think it's only a matter of time before we can take over. We have to show the world that Islam means business. We just have to keep ever lastingly at it as time is on our side," said Mohammad.

The training program ended up lasting just under six months and by that time Mohammed had been well-trained in the art of terrorism and especially making bombs and was ready to go back to America and create set ups for some major incidents.

He arrived back in America to find that his wife, Eleanor, had just had a baby so now as a father, he had renewed responsibilities, but it gave him inspiration to keep moving ahead with his planning.

He spent a lot of time with Omar explaining the training program. He taught Omar how to make bombs and many other acts of stealth. Omar was a good student.

You learn fast, Omar, I think we will make a good team.

CHAPTER 6

DEVELOPING A PLAN

"The first thing we have to do, Omar, is to decide where our first event will be. What do you think," Mohammed asked?

"Well, we need someplace where there are lots of people, don't we?"

"Yes, that's right also it has to be a place where we can get to easily enough and get away. How about a bomb in your school? That guy, the one out in Colorado, certainly did a good job. It hasn't come out but do you think he was a Muslim?"

"That's a good possibility, but we would have to have a bomb big enough for the whole building otherwise it would just be maybe one classroom. Not enough people," Omar added.

"I guess you're right," Mohammed said. "I've got an idea. How about the Boston Marathon? You ran in that last year so you know your way around."

"Wow, yes that's perfect, exclaimed Omar I can see it now. There are thousands of people there so we could get easily lost in the crowd".

"The marathon will be running in about two months so we have to work fast to get everything ready. First is the bomb"

"Omar, I know a lot about that which I learned in my training class. We have to find a fireworks store so we can get the powder and also we need BBs for shrapnel and pressure cookers to increase effect of the explosion.

That's the way they made them in my training class. We can get a lot of those things in a hardware store," said Mohammed

I think New Hampshire would be where to get the powder because there's a lot of fireworks stores up there. Let's go up and see what we can get."

It wasn't difficult. They were able to get plenty of powder and the local hardware store provided them with pressure cookers and BBs for shrapnel. They also bought some timers in an electronics store that would be used to set off the explosion. Mohammed seemed to know the answers to all the questions so it wasn't difficult to make a bomb. And Omar was a fast learner.

They decided they would use backpacks to carry the bombs and that they would set off the bombs near the finish line where there would be maximum numbers of people.

Omar knew the layout very well as he had raced there the previous year.

They went down to the location of the finish line to check everything out as carefully as they could. They knew where the line was going to be so they spotted the two locations for each bomb. They had to pace off everything to time how long it took to get from one place to another and to their car so they could make a quick getaway. They thought this was easy because they would get lost in the crowd.

One bomb spot was right in front of a restaurant where there would be a lot of people sitting out on the sidewalk. "This is just perfect," Omar: "I can hardly wait. They'll get the message that Islam is not to be fooled with"

"When we bought these bomb materials, we've ended up with enough to do a couple of bombings. How about Times Sq., New York after we do Boston? Since you were down there a few months ago you should know the layout pretty well, Omar." Said Mohammad

CHAPTER 7

MAKING THE BOMB

"Let's unpack all the bomb stuff and put it in the bathroom where we can assemble the bombs. I think we ought to make more than just one. Because the Boston Marathon is sort of stretched out, we better plant one each in different locations near the finish line. We also want to make a couple of extra bombs for Times Sq., and then we need hand grenades," Mohammed said.

"Let's see now, the powder has to be put into each of the three pressure cookers along with the BBs so we can get maximum effect as they will act like shrapnel. Also I got some nails and some bits of metal that we can add to make it more lethal. Then, we can use backpacks to carry the pressure cookers. You can carry one and I'll have the other," said Mohammed.

Now, because we want to go to New York after Boston, we better be sure the car is in perfect shape full of oil and gas. And then we'll be ready.

CHAPTER 8

LET THE COMPUTER HELP

"Mohammed I just been doing some checking up on the marathon on the computer and it looks like it's a go," said Omar. "Also I checked up on some things going on in Afghanistan and it's really terrible."

"I know, Omar, the Americans are really raising hell with our people and it makes me furious. They all seem so nice here but when they get over in our country, they turn into killers," said Mohammed.

"Yes, Mohammed, it makes me mad too. I really want to do something about it," added Omar. "This bomb will help to get the message across. I really hate these Americans. We'll show them."

"Well, Omar, when we get them at the marathon that will be a pretty strong message. You know I'm beginning to hate everybody over here and maybe when we finish with the Boston and New York bombing, we should just go home," said Mohammed.

"Okay, Mohammed, but remember when you were in your training, your friend, Ben Allie, said they want you here and you told me they really made it clear that you had no choice," warned Omar.

"Oh, I suppose so and what we are doing here is really valuable for our cause. I understand that."

CHAPTER 9

CONSOLIDATION

"You know, Omar, I think you better move in with us because with the baby it might be safer than with you living alone," advises Mohammed.

"Yes I guess you're right. Maybe I should pack up now and move in right away. How about Eleanor? Is she alright with all of this?"

"Yeah, Omar, with the new baby, we changed apartments so now we have enough extra room, so you can move in and have a room of your own. But we all have to share just the one bath."

"No problem, the only thing is I won't be able to walk to my school."

"Well, we can drive you sometimes and then other times you can take the bus."

"Maybe I'll buy a car, Muhammad."

Omar moved his things in with Mohammed and Eleanor. Mohammed was in school.

"Boy, I didn't know you had this much room," exclaimed Omar.

"Yes, and Mohammed just bought me a new sofa for the living room. You like it?" asked Eleanor.

"It really is nice, Eleanor and it's also nice to have you for my new sister."

"Well we're working at it, but it's a new world for me I'm sure you know."

"What do you mean by that?" asked Omar.

"When we decided to get married, Mohammed explained that I had to give up my Catholicism and change to Islam. I guess I have to admit that I did not fully understand the implications, but I'm learning. My priest came to my house and tried to talk me out of it, but I love Mohammed."

"Can I be of any help?" Omar asked.

"No it's just something I'm going to have to learn as I go along. I've learned that women have a different status in Islam than in Catholicism. I also learned when I went to my instructions at the mosque that a husband can beat his wife. I told Mohammed that's one thing I won't stand for."

"What did Mohammed say to that?" asked Omar.

"He wasn't too happy about that but, we'll see, and the other thing is about driving a car and going out on the street alone. There is a lot to get through in this marriage. But we live in America. One of the arguments is always is what comes first, being an American or following Islam? I think we should be Americans first and Islam after that. It's the one thing that Mohammed and I don't agree on at all: but I'm sure we'll work it out, somehow. Mohammed believes he should be a Muslim first and an American second."

"I'm sure that you will" added Omar.

"I heard Mohammed mentioned something about the Boston Marathon. Is he planning to run it with you? I know he loves to box but I don't think he's in shape for running"

"No, it's something else. I can't talk to you about it right now"

"That's just what Mohammed said. What's the big secret?"

"It's no big secret it's just that I can't talk about it right now."

CHAPTER 10

GIRLS GIRLS GIRLS

"It's really amazing, Mohammed, I'm getting more cute girls now than ever before. American women certainly are aggressive and I guess I like it. But damnit they drive me crazy. I never know what to do next when they get up on their high horse. Then they do something stupid and you wonder why bother. How about you? How do you like being married to an American woman?"

"Of course she switched over to Islam so she has to follow those rules and she has with her head covering and dress but she doesn't go along with the idea that women can't drive or walk out on the street without a man being with them. I haven't had to beat her yet. I don't think that would go over very well but then she hasn't given me any reason so it's all okay."

"We did visit her family down at the Cape where her father is a doctor. Her family was not very welcoming to me. They insisted upon asking me all kinds of questions about the 9/11 bombing in New York and I just could not seem to convince them that we had nothing to do with it. Americans are just getting the wrong story about Muslims. But someday when we take over, that will all change when we are the majority."

"Yeah, Mohammed, I can't wait either and from what I can see it shouldn't take too long with the way our Muslim population is growing. I saw on the Internet that Muslims are really taking over in England where they actually have some sections near major cities where there are large areas where non-Muslims are not allowed. Even policemen can't go into those special areas. When they wake up, we will suddenly be in charge. The banks have even outlawed piggy banks so as not to offend Muslims. That is some progress which we'll have here as we grow our population. That's the secret. Have a lot of babies and I'm just a guy that can do it. Most of the American girls that I've met are so easy."

"You think we should test out the bombs we made, Mohammed?"

"No, Omar, it might attract too much attention. Besides I'm sure they will work as I tested plenty of bombs in Chechnya during my training and never had one fail."

"Well, I'm still nervous. Everything has got to go exactly like we planned it. We can't have any slipups."

CHAPTER 11

NEWS FROM HOME

"Hey, Omar, mother's on the phone from Chechnya. Come into the living room and I'll put it on speaker phone."

"Hi, mama, this is Omar."

"Oh, my baby, may Allah bless you and keep you."

"Thank you, mama, and also may Allah bless you. It is so good to hear someone talking in our language which we never hear over here. Sometimes it gets very lonely as a result."

"Yes, my baby, when are you coming to visit?"

"Will maybe after our next project."

"What is that", mama asked?"

"Well, we are all set to do some bombing both in Boston and New York. The bombs are all made and the plans are set and it is not too far off."

"Oh, so you're making your own little jihad, I am so proud of you. We have to let the world know how we feel."

"Yes, mama, just watch the news. It'll all happen in the next couple of days and then maybe Mohammed and I can come over for a visit. Really, I would like to take the same training that Mohammed has received. Could you get in touch with Ben Allie and see if that can be set up for that?"

"Okay, I'll try to get that done very soon and let you know."

"Here, mama is Mohammed; I'll sign off."

"Hello mama, your young son is becoming a man and he is my good partner in everything I do. The only problems I have with him are girls."

"Girls? What's wrong with girls?"

"No no, mama I don't mean that it's the trouble with girls, it's the trouble with Omar being under their spell. You can imagine how aggressive girls are over here. It's not like at home. It's so different."

"Well Mohammed, just teach Omar how to keep those girls in their place like a good Muslim should."

"Well mama, I have to say goodbye and give papa our love. Bye-bye."

"It's so good to talk to mama again I get so lonesome for the family over here. Maybe we should move back home, soon, Mohammed."

"We have to get permission first. I'll check with the Imam and see how that is done. We can't move back and forth until we get permission from the top people. But first we have to get our projects completed successfully. That's not going to be easy"

CHAPTER 12

THE DAY ARRIVES

The two soon-to-be bombers could hardly sleep the night before their big day in Boston.

As the dawn arrived they were both up anticipating and reviewing the careful plans that they had made. The two boys drove into Boston in the morning in the smaller sedan car that Omar owned because they thought it would be less conspicuous than Mohammed's Mercedes. They actually drove the full length of the marathon run until they ended up around noon as the crowd was gathering near the finish line on Boylston Street.

It was the ideal day. The Sox were playing at the park. The sun was shining gloriously. It was a happy holiday and the Boston Marathon was about to run. The runners were milling at the starting line. Some were nervously re-tying their running shoes to get them just right. People from all over the world were ready to start in one of the most famous athletic events anywhere. This was a people's race, for anyone to enter. Runners were from all ages—children to grandfathers and grandmothers running in place as they waited for the starter's instructions and starting gun. The air was electric with anticipation.

"On your Mark, get ready, get set, Go" the great mass of runners burst enthusiastically ahead jostling each other as they crossed the line in this great event. The crowd roared support for their families and friends in this great celebration.

Many thousands lined the sidewalk of the 26.2 mile course from Hopkinton to Boylston Street. There were the usual signs urging the runners on and lots of people offering water and screaming encouragement. It was a gala day for Boston: one that was treasured every year. Bostonites loved their marathon. This was their rite of spring, as they love to cheer on the happy runners. Some are just in it for the fun. Others were real professional runners with international reputations.

Hardly anyone noticed that two young men with evil intent who came into the crowd from Gloucester Street onto Boylston Street at 2:38 p.m. both carried a backpack as they moved toward the finish line.

"Let's put one bomb near that restaurant and the other one a little further up. You do the one near the restaurant and I'll take care of the other one," Mohammed said.

"Okay, Mohammed."

As planned, then Omar placed his bomb near a green mailbox just in front of the outdoor restaurant. Mohammed placed his bomb about 200 yards up the road. Both of the timers were set and the two bombers moved back away from the bombs, merging into the crowd.

The crowd was slowly gathering as the two bombers casually mixed in amongst them. There were almost 6000 runners: there were women and children and men of all ages. The bombers purposefully did not recognize each other as they mixed in with the crowd keeping apart until the first runners ended over the line after 2 PM.

The time was 2:49 p.m. For one final instant, everything was almost quiet. Suddenly, the air was rent with two loud explosions, one after the other about 12 seconds apart and acrid smoke filled the area, choking anyone who was near it.

Boylston Street was turned into a crime scene, or maybe it should be called a war scene.

The mayhem was immediate. Body parts and blood where splattered all over the sidewalks. Blood covered runners and bystanders alike. Runners fell as they were hit by the blasts. Cries of help me could be heard everywhere as most of the crowd ran away from the smoke but some brave first responders ran toward the blasts to help the injured. People of Boston showed their mettle in that terrible moment of need.

Some ripped off their shirts to make tourniquets. Many had lost their legs. It was a virtual battle scene. A child was killed and two adults with over 267 injured some very seriously.

An otherwise happy day was destroyed in seconds with lifelong injuries and deaths suffered by many innocent bystanders. Boston and the world will never forget this tragic moment. The terrible Islamic message was indelibly delivered.

The two bombers walked nonchalantly and quietly away to their car and drove off. Little did they know that almost all of their actions at the scene of the crime were being photographed and soon their pictures would be flashed around the country for millions to see these two killers? A massive manhunt was started.

The largest manhunt in the history of New England was about to begin. Boston would be changed forever. Law enforcement officers from multiple agencies would quickly assemble. It was like an army moving in and many looked like they were in battle uniforms.

The sound of ambulances could be heard, screaming. Fortunately there were numerous doctors on hand as is normal at the marathon to tend to the needs of the runners. They were kept very busy in what was comparable to an emergency room triage scene.

Many of the runners stopped to help the injured, as numerous acts of heroism took place.

Oh, the horror of it all. How could this be happening? Who could have done such a terrible thing? People were asking each other. It was hard for them to believe that this was actually happening on this normally joyous day.

Boylston Street was quickly cordoned and off as a crime scene and numerous forensic examiners appeared in white costumes sorting through the liter for the tiniest bit of evidence seeking clues to how this could have happened. Forensic evidence was everywhere even on some rooftops.

The remains of what looked like a metal pot were found. These were later identified as pressure cooker parts which, we were told, would intensify the blast.

The bombs were filled with different kinds of metal, BBs and nails to act as shrapnel that pierced many of the people in the area. Some lost partial hearing due to the blast.

The city was placed under a lockdown when everyone was asked to get into their houses and stay there and not answer the door except by a uniformed policeman. All transportation was stopped in the city as well as airplanes and railroads in and out of the city.

Boston had become a giant crime scene with hundreds of police, National Guard, and firemen working to apprehend the bombers.

Later it was learned that Mohammed was already on the CIA radar having been warned by Russia of his Islamic ties. However after investigating, the file was put aside and nothing further was done. This was a lost opportunity.

With all the different agencies in Boston working on this thing, they needed a central headquarters. They picked the Central Plaza Hotel where everything was coordinated. They had over 100 analysts going over all the different evidence as it came in from many sources throughout the area.

They had to review thousands of hours of video tapes made by many different spectators with the FBI in charge of the joint terrorism task force.

They descended on the hospitals to question as many people as they could. It was the most complex investigative project that has ever been conducted in Boston or maybe anywhere in the country.

The next morning a 15 block zone had been shut down by the police. The tiniest bit of evidence was noted.

Thousands of photographs and videos were pouring in to the headquarters from sources throughout the region. There were viewed time and again to be sure nothing was missed.

CHAPTER 13

WE DID IT

The two bombers were so elated they could hardly contain themselves. Mohammed drove while Omar started to sing some song that Mohammed had never heard before.

They casually drove back to Mohammed's apartment near MIT. They didn't want to appear in a rush to attract any attention.

They were both in a celebratory mood and were welcomed by Mohammed's wife who had heard about the bombing on the television news but didn't know any of the details. She later said, after interrogation by law enforcement officials, that she didn't know that Mohammed and Omar were involved.

The bombers had no idea that authorities already had their photographs which were soon to be released and pinpoint their involvement in this terrible crime. They proved to be skilled when it came to killing, but not very skilled at planning their escape as the events of the next few days will prove.

The first job was to clean up any evidence at the apartment so that nothing remained linking them to the bombing in the event of any possible investigation. Of course that was highly unlikely as far as they thought but they just wanted to be sure.

"They are certainly going to be very proud of us at home," said Omar, "and especially your people in Chechnya will be so delighted. Now we have to get things together for New York. That will be our next hit", added Omar.

CHAPTER 14

ACT NATURAL

Both bombers decided the best thing to do would be to go right back to school with normal activities and act like nothing happened. Omar had enrolled in the University of Massachusetts, Dartmouth. Mohammed had left school on the urgings of Bosni.

Omar went down to Dartmouth to his dorm room where his three roommates were. He had one of the backpacks with him that had some fuses and empty powder tubes which his roommates helped to get rid of. These were later found by investigators who later arrested Omar's roommates as possible accomplices.

The two roommates in college were from Russia and were known to have become good friends with their roommate, the bomber, Omar. Details and photographs of the trip they all made together to Times Sq., New York is available. They are currently under arrest, in custody, accused of hiding critical evidence. They are also accused of possible visa regulations.

The two bombers had little trouble going about their regular affairs for two days following the bombing. They returned to the apartment as if nothing has happened. Eleanor was out shopping. Omar told Mohammed he was going to go down to Dartmouth to hang out with his friends, as he explained. After a night down there, he returned to the apartment in Cambridge.

Then suddenly! "Mohammed, look: look at the TV news. They have our pictures: how did they get that", Omar exclaimed? "Now we've got to get out of here in a hurry. But where do we go?"

"Well, it's time to take off to New York, they will not think of looking there," so they loaded the Mercedes with a few more pipe bombs and handmade grenades and the last pressure cooker bomb that they planned to put in Times Square. They felt they needed one more gun so they went to the MIT campus where they knew there would be a campus police man with a gun.

"There, Omar, there's the cops car". They parked and both stealthily approached the car quickly opening the back seat door and jumping in.

Mohammed held a gun at the officer's head: "give me your gun or I'll blow your head off", he said. The officer refused. Mohammed pulled the trigger and the officer slumped into his seat, murdered execution style. Mohammed tried to grab the officer's pistol and the few rounds of ammunition in his pocket that was available, but the gun was locked into the holster. After a few frantic moments of trying to release it, they gave up. They had murdered the officer for absolutely no reason.

They both jumped into their own car and as luck would have it for some reason it wouldn't start. They saw another car just pull into a convenience store across the street so Mohammed took one gun and went over to the car while the driver was in the store he slipped into the back seat.

When the driver returned Mohammed held a gun to his head and warned him to do nothing except drive over to the stalled car with Omar inside. "Okay put the stuff in here, Omar" said Mohammed.

"Did you hear about the Boston bombing," Mohammed asked the terrified driver? "Well I did that. So you better do exactly what I say because I'm not kidding. I would just as soon kill you, as look at you."

The driver quietly followed directions, terrified. When they got to the car, they loaded their bomb material and hand grenades into the rear.

They knew they needed money, so they pulled up to an ATV and obtained a few hundred dollars. Then, they stopped at a gas station to fill up. At that moment, the captive was lucky enough to open the door and escape.

In a later interview he explained how terrified he was. Sirens were screaming, it seemed like everywhere.

Mohammed took over the wheel, driving quickly towards Watertown with the police cars following. The cell phone must've given them away. Shots were exchanged.

"Omar throw some of those hand grenades at that police car," Mohammed screamed. Omar obeyed. "I think I got one car"

"I can hardly say with all the lights flashing, Omar."

"Just keep going and speed it up," Mohammed I'll keep throwing these grenades, maybe I can get a few cops."

They managed to get to Watertown after a high speed chase and by that time it was dark. Their car was riddled with bullets.

A vicious gunfight ensued with both bombers being hit but Mohammed taking more bullets than his body could stand and he went down. Omar got in the driver's seat and had to drive over his brother's body in his frantic effort to get away. The hospital examiners said that the drive over Mohammad's body by Omar was what finally killed him. Police cars followed Omar trying to escape. The car was riddled and was beginning to misfire again. Omar stopped, jumped out and disappeared into the night.

By this time there was a major police effort underway with SWAT teams on hand and dozens of police officers. Slowly the heavily armed men went house by house searching as residents were advised to stay indoors locking the door being advised by the police to allow no one in except a legitimate police officer. Search went on until late that night. Millions watched glued to their television sets as the drama continued.

The hours passed and eventually it was felt that the lone bomber may have escaped and people were allowed to come out. One resident went into his backyard and noticed that the winter cover on his trailered boat was opened and there was some blood on the cover. Meanwhile helicopters were hovering and police were everywhere.

He stepped up the small ladder and looked into the boat to find someone on the floor of the boat lying, bleeding in the boat. He quickly returned to his house and called 911. In minutes, his house was surrounded by police, guns drawn.

There was a brief moment of gunfire and then all was quiet. Police spoke over a loudspeaker that the bomber in the boat must come out or they would riddle the boat with bullets. Slowly and painstakingly, Omar came out with his hands in the air and was taken into custody by the police.

A night of terror was finally successfully terminated. Law and order had persevered and the Boston police had their man.

As an ambulance took the seriously injured Omar to the hospital, the many police cars and personnel slowly moved away from the area with citizens lining the sidewalks applauding their bravery. Boston was strong in spite of this terrible event that killed and maimed so many people, and terrorized the entire community.

CHAPTER 15

THE AFTERMATH

Omar was in bad condition, but alive. He was taken to a local hospital under heavy guard and was treated for his serious wounds.

He was read his Miranda rights by a local police officer.

"Yeah I did it, and what's all this stuff about my rights? I know my rights. I'm a soldier in defense of Allah and a hero and I want to be treated like one." Omar screamed.

"You just sit still and let us stop the bleeding or you won't ever have any rights," the officer replied.

In two days, he was moved to a local correctional police hospital where he remains awaiting trial.

Under questioning he admitted the bombing even before he was given his Miranda's rights. He has been charged with murder which will bring a death or life sentence.

His roommates were taken into custody as accomplices. They face possible serious punishment if it can be proven they were involved.

The assigned state defense attorney came to his room as Omar lay heavily bound in bandages. "Hello, Omar, my name is attorney Jackson assigned to protect you and state your position in this matter as is required by US law."

"Just get out of here: I don't need an attorney. I know what I did and I admitted it and I'm glad I did it for the greater glory of Allah."

"Well, like it or not I'm assigned as your defense attorney. How do you plead?"

"Not guilty! I'm a soldier in the army of Allah, captured by the enemy, and I know my rights."

"You probably will be looked upon by the court as a civilian who murdered innocent bystanders," Jackson replied.

"Well, we'll see what your court says after they hear what I have to say, and my brother, Mohammed, too."

"Your brother is dead."

"Oh, no, how can that be?"

"His body was heavily riddled with bullets, but the final coroner's report was that you drove over his body in attempting to escape the scene at that time. That killed him"

Omar grabbed his head as he gasped and fell back on the bed.

"Now, pull yourself together so we can get on with preparations for your trial."

"I told you how I plead, Not Guilty!" I'm a captured soldier. Don't you understand that?"

"Well, you're a captured criminal as far as we're concerned. And you're going to face charges in our court of law."

It was all the officers could do to restrain Omar, but they finally were able to subdue him to faces charges.

CHAPTER 16

THE TRIAL

The day of the trial arrived and crowds gathered at the Boston John Adams Federal courthouse where the trial of the surviving Boston bomber was held. Headlines throughout the world announced, "Boston Bomber Trial Held." The public was fascinated by the story as they watched their media with intense interest.

The courtroom was filled, as the defendant sat stiffly at the table beside his court appointed defending lawyer.

"Hear ye hear ye," the bailiff announced." "This trial is about to begin. All stand as the presiding judge, Justice Francis takes his place." The spectators and all members rose with the exception of Omar who icily kept his seat. The judge entered and took his seat as the audience also did so.

The judge sounded the gavel, "this courtroom will come to order in the trial of Omar Tarrkahn. How pleads the defendant?"

Attorney Jackson rose: "not guilty," and took his seat.

There was a murmur from the crowd. The judge sounded the gavel again. "The court will come to order. No outbursts will be permitted during the proceedings," the judge added. "What is the charge?"

The state attorney rose "It is the intent of the state to show that Omar Tarrkahn and his brother Mohammed did intentionally murder and maim innocent people, in a premeditated manner, at the recent Boston marathon. The state will also prove that this terrible act was premeditated and carefully planned to achieve the maximum numbers of deaths of bystanders through the use of explosive devices containing metal ball bearings for maximum effect that the perpetrators manufactured. It will be further proven that the defendant was assisted and/or motivated by one or more members of their Boston mosque as well as by specific training that one of the deceased perpetrators received in his home country of Chechnya under the direction of Islam."

"Will the attorney for the defense state your client's position in this case?" demanded the judge.

Defense attorney Jackson rose from his chair, "thank you Your Honor, my client, Omar Tarrkahn, pleads, Not Guilty, under his rights as a soldier in defense of his country and its people. We intend to show that Mr. Tarrkahn has been trained by his country to defend their interests wherever he may be and that the effort at the Boston bombing was to bring attention to the fact that his people are being murdered by American soldiers in several countries of the Middle East which are under the control of Islam."

The judge sounded the gavel and stated, "The court will take a 20 minute recess." The judge then retired to his chambers.

Following the recess, the judge returned and once again called the proceedings to order.

"The state may proceed," the judge announced.

The state's attorney rose and walked towards the jury box. He deliberately paused and then said "Ladies and gentlemen of the jury these proceedings will identify the accused, Omar Tarrkahn, seated before you, as the perpetrator with his brother Mohammed, of the bombings in Boston at the Boston Marathon in April 2013. We will show how these two men planned and executed this heinous crime killing three persons and maiming 280 other innocent bystanders. We will further show that they were advised and/or aided by one or more members of their local Boston Islamic mosque in this premeditated murder. Additionally, we will show that they were instructed on the technique of constructing bombs on a trip made by Mohammed, Omar's brother, to Chechnya where he resided for six months undergoing terrorist training."

The jury listened intently to the damning accusations as states attorney continued.

"Eight years ago, these two men, as children, immigrated to the United States with their mother and father from Chechnya to escape Russian persecution of the followers of Islam. This persecution, well documented over the centuries, by Russians who are principally Orthodox Christians. This has been part of a long-term battle between religions which has created an infamous history of wars to defend so-called religious rights and attempt to establish the superiority of one religion over another."

"Omar Tarrkahn was 12 years old and his brother, Mohammed, was 16, when they arrived in the United States eight years ago. They lived first in New York and then moved to New Jersey and following that to Massachusetts. Their history has been one typical of many immigrants whom we welcome to our shores. In general they integrated into our society and became good citizens. They did continue to regularly attend daily prayers at their local mosque which estranged them to some extent from their peers. The younger, Omar became a United States citizen. Mohammed did not. They became outstanding athletes in their schools and were generally regarded as, "nice guys". They were looked upon by their peers, in some cases, as a little strange because of their daily mosque attendance and their strong views about the importance of Islam. They were often called upon to defend Muslims regarding the 9/11 attack. They often told their friends that the laws of Islam were first to be followed and secondly the laws of the United States. Islamic law, the law of Allah, took precedent over US law. It was their belief that Islamic Law (Sharia Law) should replace the US Constitution. They often spoke of the oppression of Muslims in Islamic countries by our American soldiers and felt that American soldiers should stay at home. They felt that full citizenship in Islamic countries should be only for followers of Islam, not Americans, or any others".

"These two men, Omar Tarrkahn seated before you and his brother Mohammed Tarrkahn, killed in police gunfire, did plan and conduct, in a pre-meditated manner, the Boston Bombings in April, which resulted in the deaths of three people and the maiming of 280 runners and/or spectators."

"We ask the members of the jury to carefully consider these accusations and return a verdict of guilty for the accused, Omar Tarrkahn," he added. He then retired to his table.

"The state will call its first witness," the judge demanded.

"My first witness is Mrs. Jane Phillips, mother of Audrey Phillips, deceased, and a runner and the Boston Marathon," said Jackson.

Mrs. Phillips came to the stand.

"With your right hand on the Bible and your left hand raised please repeat after me: I swear to tell the whole truth and nothing but the truth, so help me God."

"I do," and Mrs. Phillips was seated.

"Mrs. Phillips I am attorney Adams, prosecuting the accused Omar Tarrkahn in behalf of the state of Massachusetts. What is your relationship in this event?"

"I am the mother of Audrey and Janice Phillips who were killed in the bombing".

"Can you tell the jury how your daughters were killed?"

"Yes, Audrey was a runner in the Boston marathon as she has been for several years in the past. Audrey was approaching the finish line as Janice, my younger daughter and I stood near it, when suddenly, as the crowd was cheering, there was a violent explosion and the air was filled with bits of metal and smoke. We were hit. My younger daughter, Janice, was instantly killed. I suffered a broken leg. My daughter Audrey was also immediately killed in the explosion as were others maimed. Many spectators were injured, the scene was like a battlefield with bodies strewn everywhere and the screams of pain could be heard." She started to weep with her head down in her lap. "It was so terrible. I can't go on," she sobbed.

"Now, now," attorney Adams murmured as he placed his outstretched hand on her bent shoulders, she shuddered, "do you feel you can answer more questions? Or do you request a brief recess for composure?"

After a long and emotional pause her sobs quieted, "no, I can go on."

"Were any other members of your family with you at the explosion site?"

"No there were just Janice, Audrey, and I. My husband, Arnold, was in the nearby store that was destroyed getting a Coke for us. He was fortunate to have sustained no injuries but he was badly shaken up."

"No further questions," added Adams.

"Will the defense cross-examine the witness?" demanded the judge.

"No questions, Your Honor."

"Will the state call further witnesses?" asked the judge.

"I call Omar Tarrkahn to the stand."

"Will you place your right hand on the Bible . . ."

"I will certainly not," burst Omar, "you can take your filthy Bible. I demand the Koran."

"Bailiff, please substitute the Quran for the Bible," demanded the judge.

"Yes sir. Do you solemnly swear to tell the whole truth and nothing but the truth so help you God?"

"I only swear to Allah"

"Do you solemnly swear to tell the truth the whole truth and nothing but the truth so help you Allah?"

"I do, but I protest this whole thing. I am a captive soldier of Allah . . . ."

The judge sounded the gavel, "the defendant will answer the question."

The Bailiff retired and the prosecuting attorney, Adams, asked Omar, "how do you plead to the charges rendered you?"

"Not guilty."

"What is your reason?"

"You know very well my reason. I am a soldier of Allah defending his faith in this country in this war against Islam and I demand my rights as a prisoner of war."

"There is no declared war between Islam and any nation in the world."

"Well, Islam is at war with the world. We have been invaded enough and oppressed by your people and many of our Islamic countries destroyed. Is that not a war? That is our war"

"First there is no declared war. Next you are not a soldier but a naturalized citizen of the United States. If there were a war with Islam, you would be considered a traitor by the United States in aiding the enemy."

"That's a lie. More of your lies as you try to control our world of Islam. It can never be. It never will be; Islam, Allah willing, will survive and will eventually take over your country, of that you can be sure."

Further accusations were made by the prosecutor who then turned the proceedings over to the defense. The defense attorney, Jackson, approached the judge and said, "Your Honor, may I speak privately to you?"

The judge sounded the gavel and said, "There will be a 10 minute recess for consultation with the defense and attorney Jackson retired with the judge to his chamber.

Your Honor," Jackson explained, "we all recognize that we are not at war with Islam and that the defendant, Omar Tarrkahn, is not a soldier. Those are facts. Therefore the plea of not guilty in the face of these irrefutable facts cannot be legitimized or recognized. I know this is unusual, but I feel under the circumstances we have no course of action other than to place ourselves at the mercy of the court."

"Further, we have tried to subpoena the Imam of the Boston mosque but he has refused to be cross examined based upon his right of risking self-incrimination," Jackson added.

"Very well, I shall take your recommendation. Let's get back into the courtroom," said the judge. The two proceeded back into the courtroom and took their seats.

The judge sounded the gavel. "The courtroom will come to order. It is the opinion of this court that the defendant's claim that he is a soldier of Allah and therefore cannot be prosecuted under international law has not been established. The defendant's admission that he and his brother perpetrated the bombing in Boston will be considered as a criminal act and the jury is charged with the duty of decision in this case."

The jury retired to their meeting room for consideration while the courtroom emptied for a brief recess.

The judge sounded the gavel and addressed the jury, "have you reached a verdict?"

"We have, Your Honor."

"Will the defendant rise? The judge asked.

"We the jury after due consideration find the defendant, Omar Tarrkahn, guilty as charged."

A murmur went up from the audience as the judge sounded the gavel, "order in the court."

"The defendant has heard the verdict; does he have any comment before sentence is passed?" Asked the judge

"My client would like to make a statement," replied the defense attorney.

"You may sentence me now, but someday you will be sentenced along with your countrymen when Islam is the law of the land. And it is coming, of that you can be sure. Your sentence will be the death of the infidel as you all are."

"You talk of Freedom . . . Freedom be damned . . . . the only true freedoms are those granted by Allah. Allah's freedoms will someday replace your worthless man-made constitutional freedoms when the world is one under Islam."

"We are the law in many countries now and we are the world's fastest growing religion and, Allah willing, the United States will soon be numbered as one where we will rule, where sharia law will replace the constitution, when peace will reign throughout the world when your militaristic policies are buried in history, when the laws of Allah will replace your man-made laws and the true fellowship of man under the one, the only religion, Islam, will rule everywhere."

CHAPTER 17

DID WE LEARN SOMETHING?

Five days of horror finally ended and Boston is trying to get back to normal. One of the bombers is dead the other sentenced by the court. Three innocent bystanders were killed, one policeman killed and another seriously wounded and 260 innocent bystanders and runners were seriously injured. All: for what?

The country will be talking about this for months, maybe even years to come. This seems to have touched the country more than even 9/11 because it was so personal. Finally the country may be coming to a greater awareness of what Islam is and what it intends to do, or tries to do, if we allow them. It is up to us.

Did we learn something from this terrible event?

Tragic though Boston was, was this the wake-up call that was maybe needed? Do people finally see the real threat of Islam and how ordinary, susceptible people can be influenced to do horrible things when they are brainwashed by an evil religious philosophy that is teaching murder and violence in their century's old effort to take over the world.

There has been much written on the subject and especially in England we find that Islam is creating terrible problems in their invasion of the English society. Is this something we see coming to the United States? Only time will tell. The warning, however, is clear. We must be ever alert. We must prepare.

The whistle may be blown on Islam who must take notice that Boston Strong is only the beginning of our resolve to maintain the freedoms that we enjoy in our country and are guaranteed by the Constitution, the Amendments, the Bill of Rights and the Declaration of Independence. Islam must not be permitted to take away those hard fought for freedoms.

But we can't sit idly by and let it happen. First we have to let our legislators know that we, as a free nation, will not stand by and idly watch Islam invade our country and especially permit the followers of Islam to occupy positions of responsibility in Washington. Though certainly there are many Muslims that are decent people, Islam is not a decent philosophy. All one has to do is read the Quran and Sharia Law to know that Western civilization cannot last in the face of such a primitive violent philosophy.

We have heard it said by believers of Islam that if you don't believe that Islam is a religion of peace, we will kill you. That would be funny if it were not so tragic.

Some in high places have been quoted as saying that Islam is a religion of peace. Even Pres. Obama has said that. However, the facts are that since the twin towers attack on 9/11, there been over 20,000 Islamic terrorist attacks in the name of Allah. Many thousands have been killed in the name of Islam. Nearly every day a suicide attack in the name of Allah kills hundreds of innocents, many of them Muslims. No one is immune from this slaughter.

There are today many active terror cells in the United States. Law enforcement is regularly weeding them out and prosecuting. It is an ongoing battle which requires our fullest support. Islam is not a phobia; it is a threat to our very civilization.

Though Muslims may appear to be peace loving, their religion demands that no one ever criticize Mohammed or Islam under threat of death. The concept of Taqqiya demands also that Muslims may lie in defense of their religion. How can anything they say be believed?

One of the problems is that we have not properly identified the enemy. We talk about fighting terrorism. We should identify the enemy as Islam, not terrorism: Islam as a theocracy, not a religion. It's like saying in World War II that we were fighting blitzkrieg rather than the Nazis.

The Boston bombing has brought this into focus. Clearly it was Islam that infected two young boys, motivating them, through religious fervor, to maim and kill innocent women and children in the name of Islam.

How many more Boston's do we need before we identify the true enemy and establish effective barriers to their insidious invasion of our Western world and our country?

Wake up America; the Philistines are at our shores.

END

ABOUT THE AUTHOR

The author was born in New York City in November 1925 the eldest of three children of Dr. and Mrs. Frank H Russell. He graduated in 1950 from the University of Colorado with a Pre-Medical Major but spent much of his life in international business as a corporate executive and CEO. He has been an entrepreneur for 40 years and is now a writer.

Corporate History

- Physicians and Surgeons Supply Inc. Denver, President
- Noreen Inc. Denver, Vice President
- Clairol Inc. New York, Group Product Marketing Manager.
- Clairol de Paris SA France, President
- Clairol Ltd London England. President
- American Cyanamid Inc. Wayne New Jersey and New York, Division Manager
- Gillette Safety Razor Co Boston, Director of Marketing

He left the corporate world in 1970 and as entrepreneur started several businesses.

- Peter Storm Limited, Manufacturer of sportswear,
- RAM Knitting, Sweater manufacturer,
- Russell Yacht Charters, International yacht chartering company,
- Bill Russell's Mountain Tours, Hiking and skiing tours in Europe

WILLIAM F. RUSSELL

William is currently concentrating on writing.

Books Published

Title	Subject
The Good Life	History of the Family
Islam a Threat to Civilization	Islam's Threat
The Boston Bombers	Boston Marathon Bombing

ADDENDUM

The dream of mankind has always been to seek and obtain freedom: freedom from unreasonable religious dogma and political domination: where all can lead lives in security and when all men and women may enjoy equal opportunity, but freedom is the key.

Before Islam can be acceptable to all peoples, it must reform its philosophy. Sharia law must be modified when such dogma as apostasy, blasphemy, totalitarian control, no freedom of speech, no freedom of religion, genital and other mutilation, honor killings and domination of all other religions must all be abandoned.

This would introduce a new dawn of freedom and would generate a new era when Islam would be welcomed by the other great religions of the world in full partnership.

William F Russell

The End